Tears in the Rain

DINA ANDREWS

Order this book online at www.trafford.com
or email orders@trafford.com

Most Trafford titles are also available at major online book retailers.

Print information available on the last page.

ISBN: 978-1-4669-4821-1 (sc)
ISBN: 978-1-4669-4822-8 (e)

Library of Congress Control Number: 2012912904

Trafford rev. 03/02/2015

 www.trafford.com

North America & international
toll-free: 1 888 232 4444 (USA & Canada)
fax: 812 355 4082

For

James and Alex
Wayne
For believing I could do it, and spurring me on to finish.
For always believing in me

Special thank you to Alan Booth for producing cover for
Tears in the Sand and *Tears in the Rain*
and
Mr Damien Horne (Jersey Occupation Museum) for loan of flag

For the six million souls who never returned from the
concentration camps of Europe. May you never be forgotten,
and may this never be allowed to happen again.

Jedzie pociag z daleka
Ani chwili nie czeka
Konduktorze laskawy
Zabrierz nas do Warszawy

Foreword

When I wrote *Tears in the Sand*, I always hoped that I would write a sequel.

I travelled by myself to Poland in 2011 to do my research for this book. I visited the Oskar Schindler Factory, Aushwitz I, and Aushwitz II, and I was extremely moved by what I saw.

I hope that this story will make people realise the plight of the children of Europe during WWII. It is a shocking story, but one that should be told in this world of Xbox, iPods, and computers.

I was moved to write the following poem after my visit to Birkenau.

Souls to Pray For

Scorched walls and beams, the stench of death
A chamber where people once struggled for breath.
Lead to what they thought was a shower,
Life extinguished with blue crystals of power.
Pushed out your train, to the left or the right
Strip to the bone, no dignity, no fight.
Language not spoken, too many to mention
It gave not a care in this camp of detention.
To think that a life could go in this way,
Thirteen hundred souls to pray for each day.

Dina Andrews 2011

Chapter 1

As the rain fell, the droplets bounced off Alex's trilby hat, which protected his face. When he had worked in the rain, there was no protection. The rain would slap him in the face, striking sometimes like shards of glass stinging his face. He looked down at the threadbare Nikkita bear. It was not the first time she had been wet and soggy.

The rain may as well have hit Alex in the face as the tears started flowing fast. His mind flashed back to the work party down at Gorey. Nikkita had been tucked down his shirt against his chest when he was working in the sand. His voice was more like a whisper when he started to speak.

"Oi Richard, such risk, such sacrifice . . . my father, my mother, my aunts uncles, and cousins!"

He went down on one knee and knelt on the grass. It took him a while. His body aged now, and it had been through a lot. He picked up the bear and gave it one more kiss. He stood up, doffed his hat, and said, "Goodbye, Richard, my saviour."

The rain eased up. Alex made his way slowly out of the cemetery, flashbacks coming thick and fast.

Heiniek, Alex's friend, had taken him out of hiding in December 1944. He was being shipped back to fight the Allied forces in France in a last-ditch attempt to defend Germany. Heniek had smuggled Alex out of Jersey and hidden amongst the stores on one of the supply lorries. He could not believe he would have to spend more time being hidden away once more.

It had not been an easy thing for Heniek to do, for he was also risking his life if he was found helping Alex. Alex was now also not as small as he once was – although malnourished, he had grown. He had been hidden underground, with no access to washing. His hair had grown long and was matted in places. His body itched with lice. His clothes no longer fitted him properly.

Alex longed to return to Poland and to find his mother and his sister, Nikkita. He wanted to feel the sun shining on his face and the grass under his feet again.

Chapter 2

Alex had been feeling particularly cold. His sleeves no longer came to the end of his wrists. His trousers came halfway down his leg. He heard Heniek on the step, hoping he was going to bring some food.

"Ah, young Alex, come with me please," Heniek said.

Alex was scared. He thought maybe he was going to be taken back to the work party.

"Do not look worried. I am here to help you," Heniek reassured him.

It was dark outside, except for the flash from the searchlight on top of the castle.

"Be very quiet and follow me."

Alex followed Heniek. They came over the green in front of the castle. There was music and laughter coming from the direction of the keep.

"They are having a party and will not notice us."

He led Alex to a little door. It belonged to a little apartment on the sloping hill that led to the castle. Heniek knocked on the door. It opened only a chink. A hand came out and beckoned them in.

"Oh, Henny, he is in a mess. Look, bring him over here. I have a bath ready."

Alex was petrified, but he let the lady peel off his clothes. She was very polite, but every now and then, she had to keep turning away, and Alex realised how much odour he was giving off.

"I'm going to have to burn them," she said, throwing them on to the fire. Little sizzling noises came from the fire, where the body lice burnt on the fire. Alex was guided into the bath. It was hot but felt good. The lady looked at him and said, "Well, now, poor love, we need to sort out that hair."

The disinfectant in the water stung his skin. He could not remember when he had last felt clean. Oh yes, he remembered. It was when he was in hospital, a long while ago.

Snip, snip, snip went the scissors as she began to snip off the matted hair. She used cotton wool and put paraffin on for the head lice too.

"Ah, now you start to look better!"

"Tank you, tank you," said Alex, kissing her hand.

"Ah, well, you can stop that. Now get up and get yourself dry." She handed him a huge white towel, which he wrapped around himself.

She next appeared with an arm full of clothes – a vest, trousers, a clean shirt, braces, socks and a pair of shoes, and a coat!

"Now hope it all fits, my love," she said, patting him on the head.

He felt squeaky clean. She was about to take his bear, but he quickly took it from her.

"No, mine . . . please," he said.

Heniek said his "thank yous" to the lady. Alex thought they would never stop kissing. The lady was crying.

"Stay safe, Henny, and make sure you look after this boy."

He waved goodbye, and they slipped away as silently as they had arrived.

Heniek led Alex down to the harbour area. He managed to squeeze him into the back of a lorry.

"Now stay there. Don't move till I come back for you."

It was quiet on the pier apart from the occasional slap of the sea against the wall, the odd cry of an unsettled seagull. Every now and then, he could hear the sound of music and laughter drifting down from the castle.

He was very cramped in the lorry, but he dared not move as the boxes that surrounded him had skulls on, which could only mean the contents of the boxes were dangerous. Plus there were guards. He could smell the occasional waft of tobacco, and he could hear their jackboots pacing up and down on the road in the chilly night air.

It seemed an absolute age, but Heniek eventually came back. Alex jumped when he heard a knock on the side of the lorry.

"Alex, it's Heniek. You will feel the lorry moving, but it's me driving. Keep hidden till I tell you to get out, OK?"

"OK," he replied, his voice trembling with fear.

He was surprised that he heard Heniek speaking Polish to some of the other soldiers.

Alex heard the engine start, but the lorry spluttered a little, and he heard Heniek swear as he managed to crunch the gears.

Alex was listening as best he could: the Polish German soldiers were planning to mutiny. They were all very angry with being forced to fight for the Germans. Finally, Alex felt a little safer.

Half an hour seemed like two hours when you are so cramped up you can't move.

Alex could hear the sound of engines and could smell the thick smell of diesel fuel. He realised he was at the airport. The tarpaulin was removed from the truck. Heniek jumped in the back.

"Quick, get in here. They will lift you on to the plane." Alex did as he was told and hid in the crate that Heniek and his friend Erik were loading on to a German supply plane.

It seemed to take an absolute age to get soldiers and supplies loaded.

Alex felt sick, and his heart started thumping as he felt the plane coast along the runway and then pick up speed, up, up, and away.

Chapter 3

Suddenly, all hell broke loose, loud noises, the smell of smoke, people shouting, and Alex felt the need to climb out of the crate. Just as he started lifting the lid, Heniek lifted him out.

"Quick, put this on, I'll help you." Heniek started fitting Alex with a parachute; it was difficult through the smoke and flames. The plane had been hit, and there was no way of knowing where they were or where some of the soldiers were as visibility was poor, and the body of the plane filled more and more and more with smoke and flames. It made Alex cough and gag.

Heniek shoved some papers in Alex's hand.

"You will need these in case you are stopped, and we are separated."

Alex quickly put them inside his coat under the parachute straps.

Alex had never been so frightened in his life, and sensing this, Heniek grabbed his hands.

"When I say jump, hold my hands and jump."

Alex looked him in the eyes and nodded; he was too scared to argue.

"JUMP!"

Alex held tight to Heniek's arms. He shut his eyes tight. All around him he could hear tracer shot, which whizzed very close to his ear. Heniek pulled a chord on Alex's chute and said, "Let go my hands."

Alex felt himself shoot up in the air, above Heniek's head. He opened his eyes to see Heniek about a metre above his head, and he felt relief that he was there. There were sparks and tracer whizzing around.

Alex hit the ground with a thud. It knocked him clean out.

Alex awoke to the sound of a crackling fire, in the distance he could hear gunfire. He listened if he could hear Heniek.

"Ah, you are awake. You did not see the ground coming, eh?"

Alex tried to lift his head, but it hurt. He put his hand on the back of his head and felt a huge bump.

"Aghh, it hurts," he complained.

"Hot tea, young Alex?"

"Yes, please," he answered and sat up slowly.

He could make out they were in a barn-like building. Slumped against the wall was Erik. His leg was twisted unnaturally, and he had a bandage around his head, which was heavily soaked with blood.

Heniek sliced some sausage with a knife, pulled off some bread, and tossed it at Alex. He caught it and ripped into it hungrily.

"Ha! Ha! Ha! It's good no?"

"Very good, I was really hungry."

"Come get your tea then."

Alex moved over towards the fire, and Heniek handed him a tin mug filled with tea.

"Where are we?" asked Alex.

"We have no idea until morning. We could be anywhere. We need to rest now for a start at first light."

Alex drank the tea. The last time he had a hot drink was in hospital, and it was hot milk. The tea tasted so good, and he felt warm all the way down to his toes. He soon fell asleep and was so cosy.

Alex was awakened by an arm falling across his body. He sat up. It was Erik's arm, but it was heavy. Alex grabbed Erik's hand, but it was icy cold. He realised that he had not made it through the night.

"Heniek, help me," Alex called.

Heniek appeared from outside, zipping up his trousers.

"It's Eric . . . He's dead."

Heniek went over to where his friend was lying.

"Yes, you are right, my friend. The tracer got him as we were coming down. We have no time to bury him. We must leave quickly."

Heniek found some sacking and covered his friend over with it. They slipped silently out into the early morning frost and mist.

Chapter 4

The sun shone brightly, and Alex had to shut his eyes and open them slowly. It had been a very long time since he had felt the sunrays touch his face. The air was very fresh, snow on the ground, and smoke came from his nose as he breathed in the frosty morning air, in and out again like a little steam engine.

Heiniek handed Alex Erik's backpack, and Alex noticed that he was dressed in normal clothes, no longer the German uniform he was wearing when they had left Jersey. Henieik also threw a rifle at Alex, and they left the area of the barn and headed towards the mountains in the distance.

It was not long before they found a road, but they kept to the safety of the trees alongside it. They had been walking for about an hour when they spotted a tank and some armoured vehicles.

"Quick, behind here." Heniek grabbed Alex by the arm and dragged him behind a stony outcrop. They watched as the convoy of German vehicles hammered along. The sound was thunderous as a tank led at the front, two armoured cars, some soldiers on foot, then two more tanks, and about four motorcycles.

"We need to keep our heads out of sight of them for a while."

It took a good half-hour as the convoy carried on rumbling into the distance before Heniek decided it was safe for them to continue their journey.

They had to find some kind of signpost soon, at least to find out where they were on a map. However, the trees were thick, and the smell of pine was strong. The wind was cold, and it started to snow. Small flakes to start with, but they just got larger and larger.

"We need to stop soon. We cannot continue. We cannot see."

There was an over-hang of rocks among the trees, and they had to rest up. The snow was now very heavy, and with the wind behind it, drifts were beginning to build up.

The light was disappearing fast, and in the distance could be heard the cry of wolves; it was an unnerving eerie sound, and Alex found himself snuggling up closer to Heniek. They huddled together to keep each other warm.

Alex awoke to the smell of woodsmoke, and Heniek was skinning a rabbit. There was a pot of water bubbling over a little fire.

"Ah, good morning, Alex." He laughed.

"Morning, Heniek," he replied and squatted by the fire, holding his hands close in to warm them up.

He sliced up the rabbit and dropped the pieces into the pot.

"We eat really soon, and then we move on. We don't want to hang around here too long."

They both ate greedily. It had been a while since the bread and sliced sausage and boiled rabbit tasted really good.

Alex went to take a pee. As he did so, he heard movement, then a snarling and growling. First, he saw teeth and fangs, then the setback ears, and the face of a wolf. He backed off very slowly. He tried not to take his eyes away from the eyes of the wolf, whose eyes were fixed on him. He walked backwards but did not see the log behind him; next minute, he was on his back. The wolf came flying through the air at him, the next thing a gun shot, and the wolf lay motionless on the ground.

"You're a very lucky boy, and this is why we have to move quickly and cannot hang around."

Heniek very quickly skinned the wolf, and he divided the skin. He made Alex wear its fur side down to keep him warm. He said it would soon dry out in cold air, and then he could turn it around the other way again. Heniek also sliced off some meal-size pieces of wolf flesh to eat later. Alex did not relish the thought of chewing on wolf, especially as it had tried to eat him! However, there was nothing else to eat, and they had to keep their strength up. They just had to hope it was a lone wolf, and they would not have to face the rest of the pack.

Chapter 5

Alex felt cold and woke up with a start. Something was digging in his back. He turned over quickly and realised it was a rifle pointing into his back.

"Get up, quickly . . . Move!" shouted the owner of the gun. The language he was speaking was Polish.

Alex looked over to see where Heniek was. He was standing with his arms in the air. He nodded at Alex as if to say "do as they say."

There were six men with rifles, and they were led into the woods until they reached a camp in a clearing. They were led into a large tent. At the table sat a giant of a man in Alex's eyes – huge black beard, fur hat, coat, and gun slings filled with gun shells. He looked up at Heniek and Alex.

"What are you doing in the woods? Who are you, and where are you from?"

Heniek tried to explain their plight to him, and the fact that he was trying to get Alex home. They did not believe Heniek, and the one in charge asked Alex to come forwards and roll up his sleeves. They all gathered around to look, and then they saw the number tattooed on Alex's arm, and then he knew that Alex had been a German prisoner of war.

"We cannot take any chances, hey? You could be German spies. But we know you are not. We are the Batalony Cholopske. You have heard of us?"

Alex looked blankly, but Heniek nodded and said he had. He knew they were a very fierce peasant resistance group. It was not good to be on the wrong side of them, or you would be dead.

The leader got up. "My name is Yanick. You are very welcome to join us, but if you wish to stay with us, you need to help with the chores." This was a very reasonable offer as there was safety in numbers. They were led to their sleeping quarters – a four-man tent, which they were to share with two other men.

"Have you forgotten what day it is tomorrow?" asked the man in the tent.

"It's Christmas Day, camp feast. Come and join us. We need sleep. It will be a good and long day tomorrow!"

They settled into their tent and were handed back their belongings and guns.

Chapter 6

There was a heavy snowfall overnight, but it was very warm and snug in the tents.

Alex lay with his eyes shut; drifting in and out of sleep, he was thinking about Richard, and what he may be doing for Christmas with his family. He barely remembered Christmas with his own family. It had been so long.

It was so warm in the tent that condensation began to drip, and it dripped on Alex's face, and he opened his eyes. The man next to him said, "Morning, Alex, I'm Stephan. Hope you had a good sleep. Merry Christmas!"

Alex sat up and yawned, "Merry Christmas, Stephan. Where is Heniek?"

"Oh, he has not been up long. He has gone to find out what your chores are for today."

Alex felt overjoyed that he was no longer a prisoner. It was Christmas Day. He could not remember the last time he had heard someone wish him a "Merry Christmas!" All the days were the same in the prison camp, and all the days in the Roman Fort seemed the same; it was also hard to tell day from night too. The crashing sound of the sea and the cry of gulls were the sounds he had grown accustomed to. It was good to be amongst his own kind. His thoughts went to his sister, and he got his bear from his coat and gave it a cuddle.

"Oi, Nikkita," he sighed.

His job for the day was to help Heniek to chop wood for the fire. Heniek insisted he chopped, whilst Alex stacked and carried the wood back to the camp.

As they entered the clearing, people had gathered around the fire. The sound of singing began, and Alex found himself joining in.

Lulajze Jezuniu
Lulajze jezuniu, moja perelko,
Lulaj Jezuniu lulaj, ze lulaj
A ty go matulu w placzu utulaj
Zamknijze znuzone placzem powieczki
UtulzeZemdione ikaniem usteczki
Lulajze, piekniuchny nasz anioleczku
Lulajze, wdzieczniuchny swiata kwiateczku
Dam ja Jezusowi slokich jagodek
Pojde z nim w matuli serca ogrobdek
Dam ja Jezusowi z chlebem maseleka
Wloze ja kukielle w jego jaselka
Dam ja ci slodkiego, jezu, cukierka

Rodzynkaw migdakw z mego pudelka
Cyt, Cyt niech zasnie male dzieciatko
Oto juz zasnelo niby kurczatko
Cyt, cyt cyt wszyscy sie spac zabierajcie
Mojego Dzieciatka nie przebudzajcie.

English translation:

Hush little Jesus, my little pearl
Hush my favourite little delight
Hush little Jesus, hush, hush
But your lovely mother, comforts his tears
Close your little eyelids, tired of weeping
Comfort the little lips, stained from sobbing.
Hush our beautiful angel
Hush, you graceful little flower of the world
Hush you most decorative little rose
Hush you most comforting little lily
I'll give Jesus a little butter with bread
I'll put a doll into his crib
I'll give you Jesus a sweet goodie
Raisins, almonds from my little box
Hush, hush, hush, you all go to sleep now
Don't wake up my sweet little child.

The sound of the singing, the accordion, the kozoil (bagpipe), and the suka echoed around. The group were cosy, and the stew was made from potatoes and wood pigeon. It tasted, oh, so good! Alex had his first glass of vodka. It made him cough and splutter, and Heniek laughed at him.

Night time came very quickly, but it had been an amazing day. Alex fell on his bed, full, and warm and cosy, and soon he was asleep.

Chapter 7

Alex was woken by Heniek shaking him.

"Alex, wake up!" he shouted.

Alex lifted his head, his eyes not quite open.

"UP . . . get your gun. We are under attack!"

The sound of gunfire could be heard all around the tent. Alex was scared. He was also unsure of how to fire his gun. He followed Heniek out of the tent. They hit the deck and kept themselves low.

"Quick, behind here!" Heniek yanked Alex by the shoulder and threw him to the ground. Heniek seemed very experienced, and Alex watched as Heniek shot dead two German soldiers.

As the last German struggled for breath, the camp was no longer in chaos, and Alex helped to carry all the dead to a mass grave, which had been dug to bury them in.

It was time for everyone to leave and push forwards to reach Poland. Tents were taken down and put into carts. Everyone helped just as equally to share the work. Horses were saddled, and the leaders of the group mounted and led the group on.

It was not quite sunlight and still very cold, and snow fell as the camp moved away. Cows tethered to the backs of the carts. The snow came down quite heavily, but they had to move on.

A young girl of a similar age to Alex walked along next to him. He looked at her and smiled.

"My name is Ania. What's yours?"

"I'm Alex," he replied.

"Where are you from?"

"I'm from Warsaw."

"Oh dear, there is not much left there now. Much fighting happened, many killed, and those not killed rounded up and sent to the ghetto."

Alex felt his heart sink – his mother and his sister, what had become of them? Alex walked alongside Ania silently, scared to talk for fear of what he might hear next. He was beginning to feel like this war would never end – so much fear, so much death, and so much pain.

Ania told Alex that she was from Krakow, and she wanted to see what was left of her family. She had escaped with her parents when they were rounding up families for the ghetto. Unfortunately, both her parents had been caught and shot, but she managed to slip away and got swept up by some resistance workers who had brought her to the group she was currently with, the Batalony Chapotskie.

Alex told her how he had spent several years on an island called Jersey, somewhere near France. He explained how his friend Richard had rescued him.

"What a brave friend you have," Ania said sympathetically.

"Yes, and I vow to go back and thank him someday if we get through this!"

The snow came down harder, and walking became a chore. The sky was black, and they knew they would have to stop soon and rest for the night.

Heniek looked back and smiled at Alex to make sure that he had not fallen behind whilst walking; Alex smiled back.

The procession soon came to a halt, and they were led to a heavy wooded area. The trees were evenly spaced, which made it ideal to pitch a tent. They were all so tired from their long walk, and such a terrible battle, it was not long after setting up camp they were asleep.

Chapter 8

At first light, all the men were called for raft-making duties, including Alex and Heniek. Heniek explained to Alex that they had crashed into Czechoslovakia. Once they crossed the river, they would be in Poland, their homeland, which they had not seen for so very long.

The men were briefed about what they needed to do to make the rafts that would carry them across the river. They would have to select the right trees to cut to make the rafts. Four in all, and one had to be bigger to carry equipment.

The woman had organised the campfire and managed to make some form of stew. Alex had had such a strange diet recently. He had given up wondering what it was he was eating so long as it was hot and filling. He was also pleased to be involved in such an important task for the morning.

Heniek was very excited. "Alex, we are almost home!"

"Yes, it has been such a long time. I can't remember too much about it!"

"Let's hope, young man, that we will both find what we have lost, eh?"

"Yes, I do hope so," Alex replied.

It had taken a whole day to plan the building of the rafts. Heniek went to speak some more to Alex, but he was sound asleep.

Alex was in a deep sleep. He was swimming in the sea with Richard. They were swimming and splashing and laughing and laughing so much.

Alex awoke to Heniek giving him a shake on the arm.

"Come on, young Alex, much work to be done today!"

The campfire was glowing, and Alex was handed a mug of tea and a hard-boiled egg. He sat with Heniek and gradually broke off bits of the shell and eating the inside of the egg slowly. He could not remember the last time he had eaten an egg. Chickens had been kept in the camp. There were also two cows which had provided milk. They had been milked for the last time that day they would be slaughtered and the meat used for food.

The women were left to pack up the camp, whilst the sound of hammering and sawing could be heard all around.

The rafts were designed so that the empty water containers and some empty oilcans could be used again after the rafts had been dismantled. All the rafts were joined to each other with strong rope so the group would stay together.

Despite the stillness of the fresh, thick snowfall, icicles bent the branches of the trees hanging over the river, which was flowing very fast. No one could survive more than a few minutes if they fell in!

Alex was quite upset, because of his small stature, he ended up on a different raft to Heniek. The weight on the rafts had to be evenly balanced. Ania was on Alex's raft, and he felt a little relieved seeing a familiar face. It was a slow process, but eventually, everyone was aboard their raft.

Alex was shocked at the speed in which they were carried along by the river, and before long, they began to see shapes in the water. At first, people thought they were logs, but then Alex realised they were dead bodies, dead German bodies, floating and bloated like balloons, showing they had been in the water for a while.

The raft at the back moved a bit more slowly, but that was because it moved around a lot. One of the larger dead bodies in the water hit the raft and made it jerk. Alex could only watch in horror as a small child of about two was thrown into the water by the bump. The mother was screaming, and without hesitation, Heniek jumped into the water and grabbed the child, passing it back to the awaiting hands outstretched to help. All was fine until the raft lurched forwards, and it knocked Heniek under the water. His body disappeared out of sight, and that was the last time Alex ever saw of his trusted friend Heniek.

"Heniek, Heniek . . . Heniek," he shouted, but the people on his raft pulled him back and sat him down. Ania sat by his side and held his shaking hand.

Chapter 9

Alex felt so numb. Heniek had got him this far, and he was so excited about being so close to Poland. He could not speak; no words would come from his mouth. Only tears would fall from his eyes, falling like dewdrops on to his coat.

Ania tried to comfort him, but even her words would not fill the hole – that gaping hole in his life that Alex now felt. What makes war worse is that bodies cannot be retrieved because it is not always possible, the risk too great, and others can be in danger. Poor Heniek's grave would be the bottom of the river bed – such a terrible waste, an enormous loss, but such an act of sacrifice to put a small child before himself.

The German bodies had stopped floating by, and the river became much flatter and calmer. They reached a bend in the river. The rafts followed the curve. A natural beach had been formed on the other side. The rafts slowed down to a halt, those who had been steering shouted for the ropes to be thrown. The rafts were moored to trees on the riverbank. Snow fell from the trees as the ropes were tied to them. The rafts were moored two abreast. A couple of scouts with guns were sent ahead to recce the area.

The scouts had been gone about twenty minutes, and they returned to say all was clear. Once everyone was safely on the embankment, the rafts were lifted out of the water and on to the land and taken apart. There was a small clearing amongst the trees, and camp was set up.

Alex stood on the edge of the riverbank, staring back-up, hoping to catch a glimpse of Heiniek . . . He did not come. One of the senior commanders had to persuade Alex to return to camp and have some food and a hot drink.

Alex held his hot tea, or something that resembled tea, and remembered when Heniek had accidentally fallen into the old fort he was hiding in. He remembered Heniek getting him a bath and fresh new clothes. Shooting the wolf dead before it had eaten him! He still had the dagger and the gun, and he held on to those as if he would never let them go.

Chapter 10

The Oder River had been savage, but now with his feet on dry land, Alex was on a mission to find his sister. They were now in Poland, but it would still be a couple of days walk to Krakow, and that was only if there were no problems on the way.

Alex had become quite close to Ania since the death of Heniek. He knew no one else in the world, apart from his family. His father was dead and so perhaps his mother and Nikkita, his sister. There can be no worse feeling than that of not belonging, and that is another thing that war does, it wrecks families.

Ania had told Alex about her parents. They had all been forced into the ghetto to live. Her father had been forced to work at the Liban's quarry. She said that it had affected him so badly; he used to get nosebleeds from being so tired. Her uncle had worked at the Baugminjer's nail factory in Gregorki. Her mother worked at the button factory on Agneiski Street. Ania's mother had seen how haggard her husband had become, and that is when she planned an escape. However, they were caught. Ania heard the gunshots but knew she had to keep running. She did want to look around, but she knew she couldn't.

Their similar experiences had brought them close, and they were both on a mission to find whatever family they could. Whenever possible, they spent time together, walking or working.

Abandoned vehicles and dead horses partially covered in snow were strewn along the roads they walked. Soon, it was not just abandoned vehicles, bodies lay frozen, some had died where fallen, and others, it was clear had been shot.

There was nothing now that could shock Alex and Ania . . . at least that's what they thought.

Chapter 11

The band of resistance fighters was becoming edgy. The closer they became to the city the more random gunfire could be heard, along with the thundering of tanks.

Behind them, they could hear tanks approaching, and they all instantly took cover.

Alex hid with Ania. He was very scared. The tanks approached thundering and vibrating along the road. They were not German tanks; they were Russian tanks; the Red Army had arrived. Alex watched as the commander jumped out waving his arms.

"You have come to save us?"

Gradually, everyone got up and walked alongside the tanks – lots of happy smiling faces. Alex was still scared. These, of course, were not his countrymen, and he knew the Red Army had a reputation and were to be feared. He had heard the men talking about them in the camp.

Alex was not, of course, familiar with the city of Krakow. Ania had to now take the lead.

"We must make our way back to the gates of the ghetto, and that's where we will find people who will know."

Ania was trying to find her uncle. She knew he had worked at the nail factory, Jozef Wysoka. He had always been close to her father and had lived in their house with them.

Alex gasped as Ania led him to the gates. "What is that?" he asked, pointing to the wall.

"But it's shaped like gravestones!"

"Yes, built to remind those of us trapped behind it that the only way out was death."

Ania looked in windows and searched in doorways, but all the houses were empty.

She saw a man scrabbling about in a bin. He was very thin and looking for food scraps.

"Where has everyone gone?"

He looked at her very strangely.

"Why, they have all gone to Oswiecim (Aushwitz)," and he went back to looking for scraps in the bin.

"Oswiecim, well, that's about 250 km away from here. We need food and water before we can even think about going."

Alex and Ania found a few more group members wandering around.

"Come, we have set up camp in a house in the marketplace. You both had better put these on, or you might well get shot."

They were handed red strips to tie around their arms to show they were allied with the Red Army. They could then be easily recognised by the liberating force. They walked with the group back to the marketplace known as Bohaterow Ghetta.

Many members of the group were requesting to visit the town of Oswiecim to look for lost relatives. So it was decided that if they could find the transport, then they would go the following day.

Chapter 12

It was a nice change to sleep with a proper roof over his head. It had been such a long time since he had felt at least a little bit warmer, and of course, Ania snuggled up next to him, so body heat also helped the situation.

The abandoned building had three floors, so the group were able to spread themselves all over the house. They lit fires in the fireplaces with some of the logs they had salvaged from the rafts. So, warm, snug, and very exhausted from the activities of the last three days, they fell asleep quickly.

When morning came, it was grey outside, and snow had started to fall. There was much activity, and everyone gathered in what was the main room in the building.

They were told that a group had been out that morning to check what was available to steal to use for transport. They had returned to the marketplace with a tractor and its trailer and an old rust lorry; all abandoned with the keys left in. They had managed to barter chickens for fuel.

When those who needed to travel were ready, they all climbed into the back of the lorry, including Alex and Ania. The lorry refused to start at first. It spluttered a little, then stopped, and would not start again. Alex and a few others jumped out to push, and it sent out a loud bang, a cloud of smoke, and started. They jumped back on and soon were on their way.

At the city edge, they were stopped by the Red Army guard, and they all had to show their identity papers. He waved them on but looked very sad when they said where they were headed.

"What was at Oswiecim that could possibly make him act like that? It's only a village!" Alex thought.

Chapter 13

It was freezing on the back of the lorry. At least walking kept you warmer because the blood pumps around the body faster when moving.

It had stopped snowing now, and the air was still and frosty. The lorry came to a halt as a roadblock had been set up. Words were exchanged, and the small convoy was waived through. However, they were now under escort. There was a strong, sweet sickly stench that was heavy in the air and wrapped itself around you like a blanket of fog.

They were led by the convoy to an area of old army barracks. Heavy barbed wire fences stood out like monstrous crocodiles with menacing teeth. Then everyone gasped. Behind the fences were walking skeletons of people. They were holding their hands out for food, dressed in blue-striped clothing. Everyone was shocked.

"Is this where they have brought our families?" asked one of the ladies on the lorry.

"Er . . . yes . . . I'm sorry," the soldier said with his head hanging down to the floor.

"We wish you luck in finding them. You may not have much luck here. You may need to go to the other one."

"The other one?" asked Ania.

"Yes, Aushwitz II, just up the road."

A group from the lorry decided to investigate further. Dead bodies just lay everywhere around. The smell was terrible. In some areas, they had been piled up six people high.

"I don't think I'm going to find Nikkita here," Alex said, looking a little green as if he was going to throw up. Ania took his hand.

"Let's go back to the lorry."

Some of the group sat in stunned silence. A lady started to sob, and Alex was shocked when her friend told them why.

"We went further in than you. You did not see the ovens?"

"What ovens?" asked Ania.

"The ovens where they burnt them. They gassed and burnt our families."

"No, no one would do that to another human!" spluttered out Alex, disbelieving what he had just heard.

"Yes, yes, they did!"

Everyone fell silent after that until they had made the 5-km drive to Aushwitz II Birkenau.

Again, walking skeletons of what remained of once healthy individuals, wearing blue and white striped clothing. Rows and rows of huts, and that sweet sickly stench was thick in the air yet again.

Red Army trucks and ambulances were all there, trying to help where they could.

They were led to the coach house entrance and met by an efficient Red Army soldier.

"You are looking for family?" she asked the group.

Everyone nodded. She split them up and found out if they were looking for male or female members of their respective families.

When it was Ania's turn, she asked about her uncle Josef Wysoka. The lady had two books. She looked in one; her chubby finger looking through the list. She shook her head, then looked in the other book. Her finger stopped.

"Gassed and incinerated." She had no expression on her face as she divulged the information.

Ania stood looking shocked. She had no more family left. Alex held her hand.

"Nikkita Zapustka," he said, his voicing shaking and fingers crossed behind his back.

Her finger went down the list. She beckoned over one of the soldiers. He nodded.

"Follow me," he said to Alex. Alex kept hold of Ania's hand, and she followed also.

"We are going to the hospital wing," he said.

Tents had been set up, and a temporary hospital area set aside.

They stopped at a bed. All Alex could do was see a small face, eyes bulging, and a shaved head. A small bundle attached to a drip.

Tears flooded down his face, and a small smile appeared on Nikkita's face. She recognised him straightaway. He was scared to hug her. She was so small and frail, and she looked younger than him even though two years his senior. She reached out a bony arm and hand to hold.

Alex looked at Ania, and she smiled back. He was overwhelmed, finally, back with a sister he could not recognise because of her malnourished state.

Children at the time of liberation by the Red Army

Chapter 14

Alex was very shocked at how he had found his sister and all the people who surrounded her.

The doctor told Alex that within the next few days, Nikkita would be transferred to the brick buildings of Aushwitz I, where a better temporary hospital had been set up.

Alex and Ania sat with Nikkita for quite some time. She was unable to speak and clearly quite traumatised. She kept smiling at Alex. All he could do to comfort her was hold her hand.

The smell in the hospital tent was not pleasant, and as much as he loved his sister, the smell of vomit and diarrhoea was foul. The occasional smell like rotten meat wafted up too, not from Nikkita but in the general area. One of the group leaders came and tapped Alex on the shoulder, telling him it was time to leave. Alex got up with some relief.

"Goodbye, Nikkita, I will be back just as soon as I can." Alex waved goodbye.

The journey back to the Krakow was solemn. No one spoke. Some people sat on the lorry with their heads in their hands. Most people were unable to find relatives. There was only a handful who had.

The mud and the stench had stuck with Alex. It was like it had seeped into the pores of his skin. He wanted to scrub it out!

Instead of the usual lively bustle of the house in the marketplace, it became very quiet. Everyone went about their chores in stunned silence. Everyone realised that with so many people now gone, the people who were left would have to be rehomed – a mammoth task that would not be easy.

Some homes that had once existed were gone or had fallen into a bad state of repair. Whole town had blown up completely. Buildings that remained were unsafe and would have to be demolished.

Ania found Alex poking the fire, just staring into space.

"Hey, Alex, at least you have found your sister. My uncle is dead . . . You have each other."

"Yes, I'm sorry, it was just such a shock to find her like that, that's all."

"It's all right. I can understand that."

"Will you help me get her better, Ania?"

"Of course, if that's what you want!"

Chapter 15

A week had passed by before the group was able to get together enough fuel for another trip to Aushwitz 1.

Ania held Alex's hand during the journey there on the back of the lorry, which started first time.

They were taken through the metal archway of Aushwitz. There were words written in German on the arch.

Arbeit Macht Frei

Alex found out later that a translation of that is:

Work makes us free

This was the German's very warped sense of humour; in the same way that they had made the ghetto wall's tombstone shaped. The Germans meant to torment its prisoners, and Alex knew all about that as he had done his share of hard labour at the hands of the Germans, shovelling sand in Jersey.

He was taken to a brick barrack-like building, which was now converted into a hospital ward. Thankfully, for Alex it smelled of disinfectant, and nurses were bustling around in crisp white uniforms.

He was quite surprised. Nikkita was propped up with pillows. Although she was still attached to a drip, she looked a little brighter. She had a big smile on her face when she noticed Alex by her bed. The nurse came over.

"Are you a relative?"

"Yes, she's my sister."

The nurse gave Alex a huge hug. "You have given her hope. She has a new strength. We thought that she did not have long. Since your last visit, she has a different look about her. You can see hope in her face."

"She is all I have left of my family. My father died, trying to escape from the camp I was in."

"It's not going to be easy, but she will need lots of looking after," the nurse explained.

"You don't have to worry about that. I will do everything I can," Alex replied.

"Stay as long as you need today."

"Thank you."

Alex pulled up a chair. Nikkita followed him with her eyes. Alex pulled out Nikkita bear from inside his coat.

"This is Nikkita bear. I have treasured her. Will you look after her for me?"

Nikkita nodded, took the bear, and gave it a hug.

Nikkita was unable to talk. The doctor told Alex that they thought it was just temporary because they knew that it was trauma that had stopped her speech. Alex wondered if he would ever find out exactly what had happened to her and also to his mother. He was happy in the thought that he now knew she was safe. Whilst she was in hospital, she would get every care she needed to make her strong again.

Entrance to Aushwitz 1

Chapter 16

Europe was in devastation, so many homeless people. Alex was very lucky. The hospital had arranged through the Red Cross, a new foster family, who had also accepted Ania too.

It was a sunny spring morning, and there was much excitement in the house. Nikkita was coming home from the hospital.

It was a lovely house in a village called Wielicza, famous for its big salt mine. Alex's foster-father worked in the mine.

The taxi arrived outside the house and hooted its horn. Alex rushed out, and he saw his sister being helped out of the taxi. He ran to her. She opened her arms, waving Nikkita bear. It was all she had with her – no suitcase, no possessions. Alex gave her a hug but was scared to squeeze her too tightly for fear of crushing her. He stood back. She was as tall as him. She had looked so tiny in the hospital bed. Her face was fuller, no bulging eyes, and her hair was growing back. She still had no speech. Alex was just happy to see her again.

She would be sharing a room with Ania as it was thought that it was best because she should not be left by herself.

The household was a very happy one. Alex and Ania had settled in well. The couple were very musical and were called Marek and Alina Bachowski. Marek played the accordion and Alina the violin, so the atmosphere was always cheerful.

Nikkita was a bit nervous. She had lost her faith in adults. Although she was almost one herself now seventeen, she really did not trust them. Marek and Alina were extremely kind and patient with her.

Alina was always giving Nikkita extra portions of food. It worried her to see her so thin, but Nikkita could not eat large amounts of food because months and months of starvation had made her stomach shrink.

Although Nikkita could still not talk, she could certainly scream the house down with her nightmares. This would wake Ania, who would just climb in bed with her till she calmed down.

It was one Sunday, just after tea, when the family gathered in the parlour. Alina began to play the fiddle, and Marek began to sing and play his accordion, which was strapped across his chest. Everyone began to sing, then suddenly a voice as clear and as beautiful as an angel began singing too. Everyone looked around. It was Nikkita singing with a huge smile on her face.

Chapter 17

Nikkita had found her voice again and was able to tell her story to Alex about what had happened to their mother after Alex and his father had been taken away.

Nikkita and her mother had been rounded up into lorries and driven to the ghetto in Krakow. Her mother had to work at the button factory on Agneiski Street. It did not pay much money, and food was really scarce. Nikkita was very small for a girl of twelve and, occasionally, managed to get hold of some eggs, milk, and cheese. She never told her mother where she had got them, but she had to steal them, which she never wanted to admit to her mother as she had done. She had to make it through the other side of the ghetto, sneaking past German posts, getting by the Jewish and Polish policemen. If she had been caught, she would have been hanged as an example or shot, but it did not matter that she was only a child.

They had been staying in a house with about four other families, and conditions were really cramped. It used to make her mother cry. She also developed a really bad cough. Nikkita said she would sometimes cough blood into her handkerchief.

The night the Germans came, she said, made her want to be sick. They rounded up people into lorries. Some people had hiding places, but the Germans would always hunt them out using informants or dogs or whatever means they could. It was mass chaos. Some people were just shot on the spot, but she held tightly on to her mother's hand.

The Germans were so eager to clear the houses. They would hurl small children out of the windows, and those who missed landing in the lorries would lie injured and crying on the streets below.

She remembered being shoved into a lorry and driven to the railway station. They were herded like cattle into a small railway truck, crammed full with about eighty other people.

Alex told her to stop for a while. He was finding it hard to take everything in. He had been badly treated himself, but it was pretty easy-going compared to what she went through.

Jews on a platform waiting to be 'Sorted'

Chapter 18

The rain poured down outside, and then the thunder started. The girls were frightened, and before Alex knew it, Ania and Nikkita had climbed into his bed.

"It was raining when we arrived at Birkenau." Nikkita offered up conversation, and Alex and Ania began to listen.

Nikkita said the train came to a halt. They were all made to stand on a small platform area. There was nothing around for miles, except a wire fence, huts, and chimneys. Instantly, a sickly sweet pungent smell hit her nostrils, and she said it made her feel sick.

A German officer in a big raincoat began dividing them up into columns A and B. Everyone was getting soaking wet in the rain, and her mother started coughing. The officer heard this and prised her away from Nikkita's hand.

"Mama, Mama," she called as she saw the frightened look on her mother's face. She was forced into the line with lots of frail-looking elderly people, people who walked with crutches. She never saw her again.

Line A, which was the line Nikkita was in, was marched towards a long wooden hut. There, they were made to strip off their clothes and then had to walk naked across to another area, where they were looked at by a man wearing a white coat. She was sent across to a line of women and children. From there, they were sent to shower, and when they came out, she was given blue and white striped clothing to put on and given a pair of wooden clogs for her feet.

Then she was shoved over to table, where her beautiful long plaits were cut off, and her head was shaved. However, the next part was worse for her. She had a number tattooed on her arm. This hurt and she cried. She got a slap round the head for crying, so she learnt in future to keep her tears inside.

Her identity had gone. She had been stripped of her clothes, and who she was at just fourteen years old. She was now just a number B6417. No mother to comfort her as she was now gone, last seen heading towards the gateway of camp B.

She was lead with others to a long hut by one of the camp privileged known as a Kapo. There were at least thirty bunk beds crammed into this room. The bunks were three deep. The mattresses were very thin on the wooden slats. Nikkita being small was made to climb on to one of the top bunks with some other girls. There were eight of them on the top bunk. "No one spoke," she said, "everyone was too scared."

There was a sudden crash of thunder, and Alex felt the girls hold on to him even tighter. Alex and Ania remained silent as Nikkita continued with her story.

Women and Children unknowingly on their way to
gas chamber 4

Chapter 19

After her first night on her bunk in the camp, Nikkita said at 5 a.m., an alarm sounded. The Kapo came in hitting all the bunks with a large truncheon.

"Get up, get up!"

Everyone was soon out of their bunks.

"You, you, and you," he said, "come with me."

They followed, not knowing what was going to happen. First of all, the girl who was a bit smaller than Nikkita was instructed to collect all the cases from the platform and take them to a shed for sorting. The next girl had to gather any other bits of clothing, pots and pans dropped on the platform and take them to a different shed for sorting. The Kapo took Nikkita to the examination shed. He gave Nikkita a broom and some sacks.

"Sweep up all the hair. Then you take the bags you have filled over to there." He pointed to an area across to yet another shed.

Nikkita began sweeping the hair on the floor into the corner. She saw her plaits and wanted to cry. She put her hand on her head and felt the roughness of her shaven scalp. Then she began to put the hair into the sacks. She managed to fill four large sacks. She put them on the trolley and pulled the trolley to the shed. A Kapo stood outside but waved her through the door.

There was a room. About six women were sat around with sacks. Two were stuffing mattresses with the hair, and the other four were sewing up the mattresses that had been already filled. No one looked up. They just carried on with their work.

When Nikkita unloaded the trolley, she wheeled it out and pushed it back to the examination shed. She could smell that sweet sickly smell, and she thought it was snowing, but it was ash. There was smoke coming from several chimneys over on the B section of the camp.

Nikkita could feel her belly growling. It had not been fed since the day before when they had been rounded up from the ghetto.

The sound of the train clickety-clacking over the line and more carriage trucks arrived. She knew she would have more hair to sweep up.

Room filled with hair, which was Nikkitas' job in the camp

Chapter 20

Nikkita always felt that what helped to keep her alive for so long in the camp was being on the top bunk. She could not be dribbled on by people being sick or suffering from dysentery during the night.

One day, a Kapo came in and asked her to follow him. He took her straight to the mattress-stuffing shed. One of the ladies was gone. She was going to be shown how to stuff the mattresses and sew them up.

A lady called Rosa showed Nikkita how to sew. The thread was thicker than normal cotton, and if you caught it taught, it could quite easily take the skin off your finger. The needle was long and thick, and if it slipped, it would also cut your finger. There were no thimbles for protection.

The food that was served up was like watery cabbage water, twice a day, a mug of ordinary water, sometimes with a hint of mud. The girls working in the shed could have the occasional sip of water from a ladle, but that was only if the Kapo was in a good mood.

It was so cold some mornings. Nikkita could barely move her fingers, but she knew she had to force them to, or it would be the walk of death to section B of the camp.

Nikkita had heard of the chambers where people who were sorted from the train thought they were going for a shower but only to be gassed in the chambers with the chimneys.

There was a terrible commotion in the camp one morning: first, an explosion which came from the area of B camp and second, loads of shouting from the Kapos and German guards.

Nikkita and the other women were all marched out of the shed. Everyone had to be counted. One of the gas chambers had been blown up. Repercussions would now take place. No one was going to admit to being involved in a plot like that.

Nikkita began to cry as she recalled what happened next. She said that the camp commandant was purple with rage. Then he began to randomly shoot people. One minute, Rosa was stood next to her; the next, she was dead on the floor. Blood had splashed on to Nikkita's face as the bullet hit her. Still shouting and firing, he must have shot about twenty prisoners. They all returned in silence back to their workplaces.

Children leaving a barrack at Birkenau after being
liberated in 1945

Chapter 21

The thunderstorm rolled out, and the girls returned to their room. Ania took Nikkita by the hand.

"You are a very brave girl."

"I'm not brave, just a survivor," she replied.

Nikkita told her that it was hard to make friends in the camp. The moment you seemed to get close to anyone, they became sick and died or just disappeared, and you never saw them again. She said the only person you could think about was yourself. It may be a selfish thing to do, but in a place like that, it's how you survived.

The food was dreadful and scarce. If they were lucky enough to have a bit of bread with the liquid green soup, it was usually stale, but food was the only pleasure to look forwards to.

The temperature at night could drop to −20, and seven people could be sharing your blanket. It was all right if you were in the middle, but sleep at either end would be difficult, and you could not sleep if someone hogged the blanket.

With all the sewing, her little hands would sometimes feel red raw with the rubbing from the cotton or where she could prick her finger with the needle.

Ania could feel how rough her hands were. Although Nikkita was now seventeen, she had been deprived of childhood years, forced to work in filthy conditions, starved, and badly treated, which something Ania thought no child should be forced to endure. Alex too had also had his childhood ripped away, spending most of it hidden away.

They were all so lucky to have been taken in by such a lovely couple who were very kind, and nothing was ever too much trouble. Food was plentiful; they had a very successful vegetable patch in the garden and fruit trees. Alex was always out in the garden, learning from his foster-father how to nurture the flowers and the vegetables in between Marek's shifts at the salt mine.

There was always clean linen on the beds, and they were, oh, so comfortable to sleep on. Nikkita and Alex had slept on floors or wooden slats for the last few years, so to be in the comfort of a bed was such a joy.

Alina was a seamstress, so she was able to make beautiful clothes, and the girls wore really pretty dresses which she made for them. Living in a proper home with regular food, soap, and water was like a dream come true for Alex, Ania, and Nikkita.

Chapter 22

In 1954, Alex and Ania were married. Alex had a job in the mine alongside Marek. It was a hard work, but he was earning a wage, which made it all worthwhile.

Ania continued with her studies and became a teacher in the local school.

Nikkita took a long while to become strong. She threw herself into art and sculpture. She would teach sculpture when she was well enough. She would have periods of depression. Hardly surprising, after all she had been through, she would write poetry to help get her through the hardest times or read books, so she could disappear into a different world.

Alex and Ania were extremely happy and had three children: two boys and a girl. The eldest son was named Richard, and the next son he named Heniek, after his special friend. Ania chose Elizabeta for their daughter after her mother.

Nikkita got married to a fellow artist. They had a daughter together, and Nikkita named her Sonja after her and Alex's mother.

There were some parts of her internment that she never spoke about. She refused requests to testify against those who kept her captive for so long when the war trials came to be.

Nikkita loved motherhood and was an excellent wife and a doting mother. She wanted to give her daughter everything she had never been able to have and, of course, lots of love and kindness. She, unfortunately, died at the age of fifty-two, from a particularly aggressive form of pneumonia; her body never having fully recovered from her childhood ordeal.

Chapter 23

Ania waved Alex goodbye as the taxi arrived to take him to Krakow airport.

Alex was somewhat nervous. He thought about the last time he had been on a plane, it had been shot at, and he had to parachute out. He remembered it as clearly as if it had happened only yesterday.

The taxi driver whistled to a tune on the radio. Alex looked out of the window. It was raining. He hoped he would be in plenty of time for his flight. He took his travel documents out, checked the times, and put them back in his pocket.

"Going far?" the taxi driver asked.

"I'm going to an island called Jersey."

"Never heard of it," he replied.

"Oh, it's an island near France."

"I've still never heard of it."

"Well, I have to fly to London, England, first."

"I see. Look, here we are," taxi driver said as he approached the arrival hall.

He helped Alex out of the car. It was not so easy for Alex to move around these days. Alex put on his trilby hat, and the taxi driver took his suitcase out of the trunk.

"Thank you very much." Alex fumbled around in his coat pocket and gave the driver his fare.

Alex checked into the desk and then was shown through security. He chuckled to himself. It was much more fun hiding in ammunition boxes and being smuggled on to a plane than have to take off half his things and walk through metal machine at customs. He struggled a little to put his shoes back on, and a lady passenger ushered him to a chair, helping him to carry his things to put on.

"Thank you very much for your help."

"No worries," she replied and disappeared around the corner.

Alex was comfortable for his two-and-a-half-hour flight to Gatwick Airport, London. Then it took just forty minutes to fly from Gatwick Airport to Jersey.

He looked down at the sea. It was beautiful and sparkling, just as he had remembered it.

It did not take long for his luggage to arrive, and he was able to wait for the number fifteen bus to take him to the Liberation bus station in St. Helier. His hotel was the Dolphin Hotel in Gorey right on the pier near the castle. He waited for the number one bus, and in thirty minutes, he was in Gorey.

He was very surprised that it had hardly changed from when he had last been there. The railway line had gone, but it very looked the same. It was very sunny, but clouds were building up across Grouville Bay.

He booked into the reception of the hotel. Alex knew that the next day, he would go down to the village to an address he had scribbled on a piece of paper.

It was a strange feeling to be free, where he was once prisoner and had to hide. He looked out of his room window, across the bay, to where he had once shovelled sand. Rain started to fall against the windowpane, and tears began to fall down Alex's cheeks.

About the Author

My inspiration for writing *Tears in the Rain* was as a follow-on to the previous book I have written called *Tears in the Sand*. I also have a degree in English literature and history, so I have combined my knowledge of both subjects to write these books.

I have worked in special education for thirteen years and noticed that there was not much available on this subject for nine- to twelve-year-olds and decided to have a go at writing.

I also battled with a brain tumor last year, but also managed to get the first book published and carry out research for the second, by visiting Poland on my own.

I live in on the island of Jersey in the Channel Islands, which is part of the British Isles. I have two sons James and Alex.

inted in the United States
Bookmasters